Library of Congress Cataloging in Publication Data: Dubowski, Cathy East. Escape to third earth. On t.p. the registered trademark symbol "TM" is superscript following "Thundercats" in the title. SUMMARY: When their planet is destroyed and their spaceship damaged, the Thundercats chart their course for the third planet from the sun in the Milky Way galaxy where they hope to find asylum. 1. Children's stories, American. [1. Science fiction] I. Fernando, ill. II. Starr, Leonard. III. Title. PZ7.D8544Es 1985 [Fic] 85-1990 ISBN: 0-394-87467-6

Manufactured in the United States of America   1 2 3 4 5 6 7 8 9 0

Escape to Third Earth

A ThunderCats Adventure

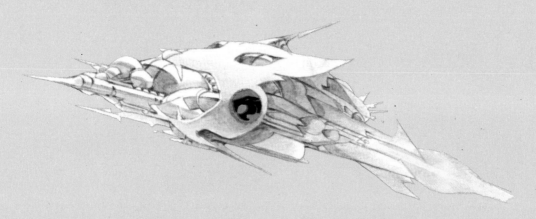

by Cathy East Dubowski
illustrated by Fernando

adapted from the teleplay
by Leonard Starr

Random House New York

Deep in space a small caravan of ships was beginning a grim journey into the unknown. Many of the travelers looked back—some bravely, others tearfully—at a once beautiful planet that now glowed and pulsed horribly in the growing distance.

Six Thundercats gathered solemnly on the flight deck of the flagship to stare at the image of the planet on the telescreen. There was the elder, Jaga the Wise; Panthro, master of martial arts; Cheetara, the swift one; Tygra, master of camouflage; and the mischievous little ones, Wilykit and Wilykat. All knew the end was near.

"I suppose I should awaken Lion-O," said Tygra. But as he turned to go, Cheetara blocked his passage.

"No!" she cried. "Why upset the boy needlessly?"

Jaga settled it. "We will wake him. If Lion-O is to rule one day, he must learn to take the bad with the good."

"You see, Cheetara?" said Tygra. "Jaga is right."

A voice full of mischief mocked from across the room. "Jaga is right, Jaga is right," said Wilykat, scooting about. "Jaga is *always* right!"

"Not always," said Panthro. He reached out with his muscled arm and grabbed the boy, hoisting him into the air. "If he was, he would have left a little troublemaker like you behind!"

"*Panthro's* right!" squealed Wilykit, dancing around the wrestling pair.

Jaga raised his hand. "We will have no squabbling! Especially today! Cheetara—fetch the boy!"

Within minutes Cheetara returned with Lion-O. Snarf, a bearded, chubby little creature with a long tail, bustled in behind them.

"Why are you waking the boy?" complained Snarf. "Nothing is as important as a young boy's sleep!"

"You old nanny!" teased Cheetara.

"Easy for you to say!" replied Snarf. "You're not responsible for Lion-O's welfare. I am! Just let him come down with rocky asteroid fever or the purple pip, and who gets blamed? Poor old Snarf, that's who!"

Jaga motioned for silence and held out his hand to the boy.

"What's going on?" asked Lion-O. He yawned.

Jaga pointed to the telescreen. Suddenly a mighty explosion rocked the ship, and the image of the planet rumbled and at last erupted into a million fiery fragments that illuminated the darkness.

"What was that?" cried Lion-O.

"That was Thundera," said Jaga. "The planet we used to call home."

Lion-O stared in disbelief, trying hard to hold back the tears. Jaga stroked the boy's head.

"Yes, Lion-O. Thundera is gone now," said Jaga. "But the Code of Thundera will live on in your heart. Your sacred duty will be to rule according to that code in our new home, wherever that may be. Justice, Truth, Honor, Loyalty—"

"I will, Jaga, I swear it!" cried Lion-O. "I mean, I-I'll try . . ."

"I know you will," Jaga said kindly. The responsibility was great

for one so young. But Lion-O would have the other nobles—
Panthro, Tygra, Cheetara, even Wilykit and Wilykat—to teach him
the skills he would need to rule wisely.

"There is something else you must see," said Jaga. "The most
important part of your heritage." Jaga led the boy down a long pas-
sageway to a silent chamber. In the room stood a low platform with
an ornate stand at its center. On the stand was a magnificent
sword. With Jaga leading him, Lion-O approached it, his eyes full of
wonder.

"This," said Jaga, "is the Mystic Sword of Omens. It holds the
source of all our powers—the Eye of Thundera!"

Lion-O's hand seemed drawn to the beautiful object. And as soon as he lifted the Sword, it began to glow, filling the room with light. Above his fingers the crossbar curled. Then suddenly—*the Sword began to grow!* Shining, the blade rose up to one, two, *three* times its original length, until at last it became too heavy for the boy to hold aloft. The tip fell and struck the floor with a mystical chiming sound.

"Jaga—the Sword is alive!" Lion-O cried fearfully.

"Yes," said Jaga. "But do not be afraid."

"What are these holes?" asked the boy. "And where is the eye?"

Jaga pointed to the crossbar. "The Eye of Thundera is here, but it sleeps until needed. And those are not merely holes. Looking through those magic apertures will give you sight beyond sight. They will show you dangers that lie in wait for you—even before you face them."

"How do I wake the Eye?"

"You will not need to," said Jaga. "The Eye will know when it is needed. Even before *you* do."

Then Jaga called the others into the chamber. "The Sword of Omens," he told them, "will serve Lion-O, as hereditary Lord of the Thundercats. And through him, it will serve each of you as well."

Suddenly the ship lurched and tilted violently, nearly knocking the Thundercats off their feet.

"We're being attacked!" cried Panthro.

"Lion-O! Remain in the Sword Chamber!" shouted Jaga.

"No!" cried Lion-O. "If there's going to be a fight, I think I should—"

"Do not argue!" Jaga's voice was stern. "Snarf! Look after the boy!"

In seconds Cheetara had streaked to the controls on the flight deck. "Look!" she cried to the others as they raced in behind her. She pointed to the telescreen.

Mutants—from the planet Plun-Darr! For centuries they had harassed the peaceful planet of Thundera with threats of war. Now they pursued the homeless Thundercats across the galaxy. But there was something curious about the ships. Each bore the emblems of *three* tribes from Plun-Darr—that of the Reptilians, the Jackalmen, and the Monkians.

"They've always been at war among themselves!" said Tygra. "Can they really be attacking us together?"

Jaga's face hardened with anger. "They must have joined forces in a desperate attempt to seize the Eye of Thundera!" Quickly he signaled the other ships. "Assume defensive formation!"

The caravan of Thunderian ships curved into a giant circle and prepared to fight. But these were ships of peace, not of war. When the people of Thundera had hastily fled their doomed planet, they had crowded onto their ships with as many supplies as possible. There had been little room for weapons. Now the tiny flashes from their guns were puny compared with the merciless blasts fired by the Mutants' formidable battleships.

"We're losing them, Jaga! We're losing all our ships!" shouted Panthro.

The Thunderian nobles watched helplessly as one by one the Thunderian ships were blasted away. Finally only the flagship was left.

Zzzaaappp! The flagship shook. Zzzaaappp! Zzzaaappp! The Mutants had attacked the Thundercats' ship with grappling rays! Like the long encircling tentacles of an octopus, the rays stuck to the flagship and drew it closer and closer to the Mutants. Within minutes, Mutants were swarming into the Thundercats' ship.

Quickly Panthro somersaulted into the middle of the mob. Using every karate chop, kick, and punch he knew, he sent the ugly creatures flying. A Monkian and a Reptilian aimed threatening blows at Cheetara, but she dodged them so fast that she seemed to be a blur—and the two Mutants knocked each other out! Tygra, master of camouflage, kept a whole gang of attackers guessing by blending into the wall and then reappearing behind them. Wilykit and Wilykat added to the confusion by scampering around the room throwing smoke pellets that sent the intruders into fits of sneezing.

But the real danger lay elsewhere in the ship. The slimy Reptilian S-S-Slithe was leading a small band of Mutants in search of the Sword of Omens! Finally they burst into the Sword Chamber. There, standing bravely in the middle of the room, was Lion-O, his small hands grasping the great Sword. The loyal Snarf leaped heroically at S-S-Slithe's throat, but a Jackalman fired a strange rifle that shot out a huge net and trapped him.

"Now, boy," S-S-Slithe said sleekly. "Give me the S-S-Sword."

"You shall not have it while I live!" cried Lion-O.

"S-s-so! I won't have long to wait!" S-S-Slithe said with an evil laugh. He reached for the Sword, but suddenly it began to glow and vibrate in Lion-O's hand. The sleeping Eye of Thundera snapped open and unleashed a mighty roar as it flashed a beam of light that bathed the room in an intense red glow. Then the Sword grew to its full majestic length. As Lion-O struggled to hold on, the Sword— under its own power—began to whirl about his head, slashing menacing figure eights in the air. The power of the Sword so terrified S-S-Slithe and his small band of Mutants that they tripped and stumbled over one another in their haste to flee.

"Back to the s-s-ship—and hurry!" shouted S-S-Slithe as he streaked through the battle on the flight deck. The Mutants thronged back into their own ships, withdrew the grappling rays, and were soon zooming into space.

The combat-weary Thundercats looked at one another in surprise. "What was *that* all about?" said Tygra.

Then they turned, and there stood Lion-O, his eyes wide in amazement, holding the Sword of Omens.

"You're not hurt, are you?" asked Jaga, grasping the boy by the shoulders.

"No," said Lion-O. "Snarf got a few bruises, but I managed to hold them off!"

Then Jaga took the Sword. "You did it with the Sword of Omens?"

"Well," Lion-O said sheepishly, "actually . . . the Sword kind of did it for me, I guess. . . ."

"I see," said Jaga, holding back a smile. "You were very brave indeed, my young lord."

A few hours later the Thundercats assembled on the flight deck for Panthro's report.

"Our ship has been severely damaged," he said. "We'll never be able to make it to our original destination." He flashed a map up on the telescreen. "The best we can do is this little galaxy called the Milky Way. I've run a galactic scan for atmospheric compatibility. The third planet out from the sun"—he pointed to Third Earth—"gives me a readout of about ninety-six percent."

Lion-O was puzzled. "Atmospheric compati—what?"

"It means we can breathe the air," explained Tygra.

Jaga fed some additional information into the computer. He frowned as he read the results. "The planet is still light-years away. Our only chance is for all of you to make the rest of the trip in the suspension capsules. They will drastically slow down the aging process. Otherwise we will all perish in space before we can get there. I," he added slowly, "will pilot our ship to the blue planet."

"No, Jaga!" cried Cheetara. "Without suspension, you'll die! We'll use the robot pilot!"

Jaga shook his head. "In the ship's damaged condition, it must be piloted manually for as long as possible—or we cannot be assured of reaching our destination."

"We can't be sure of that anyway!" said Tygra. "Why not take our chances—together?"

Jaga looked around affectionately at each troubled face. "I am by far the oldest," he said quietly. "Even with suspension, some aging will take place. So either way I would not live long enough to complete the journey. Now—let's have no more talk!"

Solemnly the Thundercats said good-bye to Jaga and took their places in the capsules.

But Lion-O threw his arms around Jaga's neck. "I'm afraid, Jaga. What will I do without you?"

"You must be brave. It is your duty."

"I-I will, Jaga—for *you!*" the boy said tearfully.

Jaga tucked Lion-O into his capsule. "The Eye of Thundera will be waiting for you when you reach your new home. And I will always be with you . . . in spirit." Then he kissed the boy on the forehead and closed the hatch. It would be a long, lonely voyage for Jaga. "I only hope our calculations are correct," he thought as he activated the suspension capsules. Then he placed the Sword of Omens next to Lion-O's capsule. The young boy was going to need every ounce of its power as he learned to be Lord of the Thundercats in a strange new world.

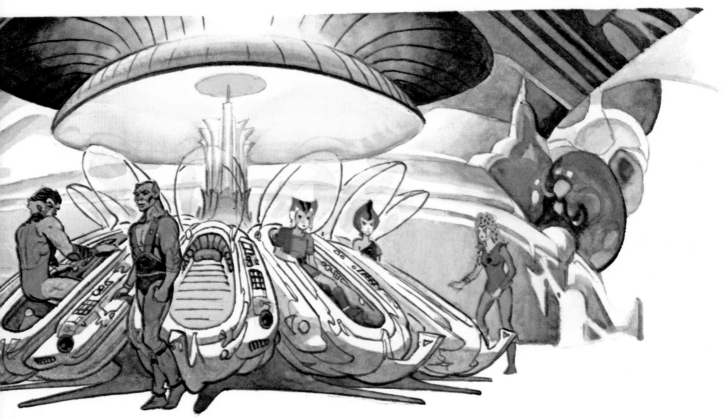

It was many light-years later when Snarf poked his furry head out of his suspension capsule and looked around. He rubbed a big bump on his head and winced. "I *knew* I wasn't going to like this!" he whined. "Where am I?"

He was no longer in space, but in a strange, lush jungle. Nothing moved except a few thin curls of smoke rising from the wreckage of what used to be the flagship. "We must have crashed!" he exclaimed. Then he began a frantic search for Lion-O's capsule. Finally he found it and opened the hatch. But instead of a little boy, a tall, muscular young man sat up and looked around, confused.

"What . . . ? The suspension capsule . . . how did it get so small? And Snarf, you look smaller too. What's going on?" Lion-O climbed awkwardly out of the capsule and walked to a nearby pond. He knelt and looked at his reflection in the water. "Why, I've grown!" he exclaimed.

But suddenly a large, dark shadow fell across the water.

"Look out!" cried Snarf. "Mutant ships—they're back!" He and Lion-O ducked into the bushes. Seconds later the Mutants teleported down into the clearing.

"S-s-search carefully!" shouted S-S-Slithe. "The Eye of Thundera must be here somewhere!"

"Look!" cried a Monkian. "The Thundercats are in suspension capsules!"

"Hnyah, hnyah!" sneered a Jackalman. "We'll never have a better chance to get rid of them forever!" He raised his spiked club into the air.

Lion-O shook his head. He couldn't quite remember who the Mutants were, but somehow he knew that those capsules contained something important. "Stop!" he cried as he swung out on a vine and knocked the Jackalman's club away. The Mutants turned on Lion-O in fury. He tried to fight them off, but he was outnumbered. They flung him back into the bushes. As he fell, his hand touched the hilt of the Sword of Omens, which was lying half hidden in the underbrush. Immediately it began to glow. "This sword . . ." said Lion-O, trying hard to remember. "I know this sword . . ."

Suddenly a vision of his beloved Jaga appeared before him. "J-Jaga—is it really you? You're still with me?"

Jaga smiled. "Yes, I will always be with you. Pay heed, now, for it is your destiny that you hold in your hand, and the source of the Thundercats' power. Remember, gazing through the eyeholes of the Sword will give you *sight beyond sight.* . . ." Then the vision was gone.

Lion-O did as Jaga had instructed him, and the power of the Sword helped him remember everything. He knew he must save the other Thundercats, who still lay sleeping peacefully in their capsules. Quickly he held the mighty Sword aloft and cried,

"Thunder-Thunder-Thunder-Thundercats—Ho!" The Sword tripled in size. Then the Eye snapped open with a furious roar, flashing the glorious Thundercat symbol into the darkening sky.

Instantly Lion-O's fellow nobles awoke from their capsules and sprang into battle with the Mutants.

"Panthro, look who's joined us!" called Cheetara, pointing to the dueling Lion-O.

"Well, well. He's grown some, hasn't he?" Panthro said as he easily tossed a Jackalman over his shoulder. United, the Thundercats began to overpower the Mutants.

"Back!" shouted S-S-Slithe. "Teleport yourselves back to the s-s-ship!" The Mutants pressed glowing buttons on their belts. Mysterious beams shone down from their ships, and they were gone.

"That takes care of them!" said Wilykat.

But Panthro wasn't so sure. "They'll be back. They'll never rest until the Eye of Thundera is in their clutches!"

"That will never happen!" insisted Lion-O. "*I* will not allow it!"

"Get him," snickered Wilykat. "One little skirmish, and he thinks he's a hero!"

"Now, now," said Tygra, clapping the young lord on the back. "He did a pretty good job his first time out."

Panthro began to look through the wreckage of their ship. "Now all we have to do is figure out how to survive in this place!"

Lion-O struck a heroic pose. "We *will* survive—and create a mighty empire. I, Lion-O, Lord of the Thundercats, proclaim it!"

"Oh, brother!" said Wilykit, giggling, and the other Thundercats began to chuckle. Lion-O blushed. Though he'd grown tall and manly during their long journey to Third Earth, he had not received the education of a young Thunderian noble and was still like a little boy in many ways. He had much growing up to do.

"Um, I mean, with the help of all of *you,* of course," he added. The Thundercats broke out into good-natured laughter that seemed to fill the strange gathering darkness with the sound of home.

The next day the Thundercats began to make plans for their new lair. Not far away, a single shipful of Mutants were also making plans. They, too, had decided to settle on Third Earth—at least for now—and they were scouting for a place to build their own fortress. Then they would devise new schemes for seizing the Sword of Omens. As they cruised low over the alien terrain, they saw luxuriant vegetation and great bodies of water—but no signs of habitation. Once they thought they saw a beautiful city, but as they flew nearer they could see that the once grand buildings now lay in ruins.

Then the Mutants saw an ominous onyx pyramid towering into the sky. At the four corners were tall, thin pillars, and from their pointed tips crackled four bolts of lightning that joined at a point above, forming a canopy of pure energy over the pyramid.

"No primitive life form built that!" said one of the Monkians. "I don't like the looks of it!"

"Neither do I!" said S-S-Slithe. "Let's-s-s get out of here!"

But before they could escape, the four fingers of lightning reached up to surround the ship and smash it to the ground. As the dazed Mutants crawled out of the wrecked ship, a side of the pyramid seemed to vanish, and a dark voice roared out: "Ennterr!"

Almost against their will, the Mutants were drawn into the forbidding structure. A glowing sphere of light led them down murky passageways whose walls were etched with ancient hieroglyphics. Soon they came to a large, dimly lit chamber. Against the far wall stood a mummy case flanked on both sides by fierce half-man, half-beast statues. Nearby a black cauldron bubbled eerily.

Again the voice roared, filling the room: "As long as evil exists—Mumm-Ra lives!" The casket creaked open. Out stepped a grotesque, decrepit figure, wrapped in decaying rags and wearing a long, hooded red cloak.

"W-w-what s-s-sort of being are you?" asked S-S-Slithe, trembling.

"I am Mumm-Ra . . . and I know of your mission here on Third Earth: You wish to capture the Sword of Omens, which cradles the Eye of Thundera!"

"You know of it?" asked one of the Jackalmen.

Mumm-Ra smiled, his red eyes glowing like hot coals. "I have known of its power for thousands of years . . . from the time when this was still First Earth. Now, together we can make it our own!"

S-S-Slithe snickered. "What makes you think we need *your* help to get it?"

"You dare to mock my power?" cried Mumm-Ra. He hobbled to the cauldron. "Come, look at your ship."

A thick cloud of vapor rose from the boiling black waters, and in it the Mutants could see an image of their damaged vehicle. Suddenly the sands opened up and swallowed the ship forever!

"Our communicators!" all the Mutants cried at once.

"Now you are stranded on Third Earth," taunted Mumm-Ra. "Cut off entirely from your people. Without me, you will perish."

He pointed to the cauldron once more. In the rising vapors, they saw an image of Lion-O. He was strolling in the woods, parrying playfully with the Sword of Omens. On his left hand he wore his powerful, shining glove, the Claw Shield.

"Now," Mumm-Ra cackled, "you shall see my full power!"

He stretched his bony arms to the heavens, and lightning crackled from his fingertips. "Ancient spirits of evil"—his bent figure began to grow—"transform this decayed form"—his muscles ripped through the bandages—"*into Mumm-Ra the Ever-Living!*"

The Mutants fell back in fear. Before them stood a frightening monster with the wings of a vulture and the jaws of a mad beast. A red light pulsed on his chest, revealing the sinister emblem of a double-headed snake. With a swirl, Mumm-Ra disappeared.

Deep in the forest, Lion-O's sport was suddenly interrupted as the Sword of Omens signaled danger. The young lord gazed through the eyeholes of the curled crossbar, but before he could see anything, he was surrounded by an odd sound, like the rustling of swirling leaves. He turned, and Mumm-Ra appeared out of thin air. Lion-O started to summon the other Thundercats—but then he changed his mind. "I must prove that I am worthy to be Lord of the Thundercats," he said to himself. "I must face this demon alone!" But as he raised the Sword to strike, the flapping of Mumm-Ra's vulturelike wings sent it flying into the air. It landed in a black tar pond. The nimble youth dashed to the edge and just managed to grab the hilt of the Sword before it sank.

"I was wrong—I must try to call the Thundercats!" said Lion-O. But sticky black goo completely covered the Eye of Thundera—and Lion-O could not summon its power.

Mumm-Ra roared with laughter. "You think to destroy Mumm-Ra the Ever-Living? It cannot be done, boy!" He fell upon Lion-O and pinned him to the ground, enveloping him with his massive wings. His eyes were full of anticipation—the Sword of Omens would now be his! What wondrous evil he could unleash across the universe with this glorious Sword in his grasp! But then Lion-O held up his Claw Shield. Mumm-Ra gasped and pulled back, for in the glove's shining surface, he saw the reflection of the evil in his own glowing red eyes. Terrified, he fled into the sky. The other Thundercats charged into the clearing just in time to glimpse the monster before he completely disappeared.

"Look!" cried Wilykat. "What was that?"

Lion-O got to his feet. "He called himself Mumm-Ra the Ever-Living. He was ferocious, and he seemed to fear nothing. Yet the

reflection of the evil in his own face drove him away."

"You showed great courage by facing such a devil alone," said Tygra.

"But I should have summoned the rest of you from the very beginning," admitted Lion-O. "Together we are much stronger than even the worst evil in the universe."

Cheetara smiled. "I think Lion-O is growing up," she said. And they all joined in to give him a rousing Thundercats cheer.

But as the Thundercats headed back to their temporary camp, Wilykit tugged at Lion-O's arm. "Do you think that awful Mumm-Ra will ever come back again?" she asked.

"I don't know," said Lion-O, gazing up at the sky. "I just don't know." To the southeast, lightning flashed. "Looks like a storm's brewing," he added.

But it was not ordinary lightning. It flashed only above the Black Pyramid. Inside, a furious Mumm-Ra had returned to the hushed darkness of his crypt.

The tomb echoed with his words: "Thundercats, I have not finished with you yet! There will be another time...."

29